THE THEATRE

FOREWORD

This is dedicated to my friends and community in Kansas, for when we have the opportunity to make a movie together. To the ghost with the most who has inspired so much positive change in me, I'm glad you're alive.

For Kansas City in general who is the real Clatter City. For Theatres around the world that act like lighthouses for lost souls like myself. Your magic is some of the only true magic we ever really get in life. Thank you.

CHAPTERS

CHAPTER ONE

1990

A metal head danced along a dark path in the woods. Clunky plastic headphones sticking out like antennae attached to rapidly spinning CD player. Mandy shook her shaggy hair violently, the music so loud it could be heard perceptibly around her.

"Collector!

In the light of

the red moon!

Collector!"

She sang along, stomping around energetically. The motion made her cd come loose, spinning out, leaving her with the sound of shaking metal. She stopped, pouting, intense energy on pause as she put it back on track. Hearing a twig snap she looked up pulling her headphones down, listening.

"Hello?"

Brush rustled making her jump.

"Seriously, is someone there?" Irritably blowing a big, white, bubble with her gum she stood over confidently. Hearing something move quickly behind her she spun around. The bubble popped.

"I'm really not one to be fucked with!" She called out, chewing, continuing her walk. "Mess with me at your own ri…"

A smiling, plain faced, blonde man in a tight skeleton suit walked out of the night holding an off white dagger.

"You know…" He said, looking like a disembodied head who's form had lost it's flesh. "There are twenty-two bones in the human skull."

Mandy took off running, dropping her CD player, the skeleton man behind her. She wasn't fast enough, grabbing her by her shaggy hair he ripped her backwards. Struggling grabbing for his hands, his knife cut into her neck, sawing and serrating until it was fully severed. Her body fell to the ground as he raised her decapitated head into the air

"*Collector,*

in the light of

the red moon

Collector"

Played behind them from her blood covered headphones.

"Ugh."

Clive sat inside of the projector booth watching "Bone Demon" from his small window for the fiftieth time that month. People were going crazy over this one, biting at the doors every morning to watch the new premier slasher.

Seeing the same movie over and over, no matter how good it was, made him feel claustrophobic. He tossed some popcorn in the air trying to catch it with his mouth and succeeded, crunching egotistically. He should have been sick of the stuff, his diet eighty-five percent corn and butter. Probably in his blood at this point, but at least he was getting his daily fiber intake.

He looked down into the audience. The dark shape of a woman jumped clinging to her laughing boyfriend who pulled her in for a kiss. He frowned, he'd gotten into a fight with Gwen before he'd left the house earlier. She was mad he had to work again, not like running a business left you much down time. He'd obviously wanted to hang out with her over watching this five more times and having popcorn for dinner.

Hearing a whirring next to him he observed the screen slowly shudder through multiple scenes of death before white spotted burns fractured across their screaming faces. The film went off track flapping against the back of the camera, people inside the theatre groaned.

"Put the movie back on!" A man yelled from the audience.

Flustered, he jumped into action to stop the projector but it was shaking, screaming. A small explosion ricocheted a piece of metal into the wall and with a gentle poof, a flame was born.

"Oh fuck."

He ran to the side throwing his water onto the fire only to have it surge upwards.

"Oh no. Oh no."

Doing a useless panic dance back and forth he took the flannel from his waist throwing it repeatedly onto the flame only to have it raise to the ceiling. Realizing the fire was out of control he ran to the door grabbing the handle finding it was locked.

"What the fuck?" He jiggled the knob but it wasn't moving. He pounded on the door. "Hey! Guys! Guys!"

He yelled but it wouldn't budge. He tried to kick it down, the place was built in the 1920's, stronger than steel. Running to the projector window he knocked it out. Smoke billowed into the theatre room, angry people leaving screamed.

"Help! Fire! Fire! Help!" He shouted.

People started running, he leapt back as the flame encompassed the wall. It bled out the window, greedy tendrils spreading like an infection. Clive beat against the door, hands going red, skin tearing. He felt heat sweating him through his jean jacket, molten lava licking at his shoes. He screamed, no one hearing him as the fire went higher, his skin boiled and popped, dark hair going up in flames

Everything went cool, he felt like he was floating, laying on his back in a formless, black, lake. Red and blue lights flashed around him, his chest ripped open, someone was vacuuming his insides. A sky, Gwen's crying face, black figures, moist heavy soil, dirt, anger, rage. A skull laughing, thousands upon thousands of bones, tv screens playing something wrong, a jagged white knife slashed through the darkness, a girl screamed.

His eyes opened, back in the projection booth. He pat himself down, finding his jeans, **HORROR** shirt and jean jacket untouched, skin smooth and unbroken. Had it been a bad dream? He laughed in relief.

"Man, I've had some messed up nightmares before but…" His chuckle died in his throat. The room looked different, brighter, freshly painted. He bent down looking at a projector he'd never seen before. "Wow, this looks brand new. What is that?" He reached out to touch a round shape where the film should be and his hand went right through it. "Ugh!" He pulled it back out and staring, before putting it back in and pulling out again. "Whaaaat…?"

At once he was standing in the lobby surrounded by people. He tried to push his way through the crowd, but found he just walked right through them. He yelled at a man.

"Hello? Hello?"

"It's freezing in here." The guy said to his wife, rubbing his shoulders.

A painful frown etched into his face as he found his way to the center of attention. Mouth dropping open in shock he saw Gwen and his business partner kissing, her dressed in white.

He shouted out and a lightbulb above the bar burst, Marina the blue haired bartender screamed, everyone turning to look. He popped outside into the rain standing next to the ticket booth beneath the marquee that read,

GWEN AND HUNTER

MARRIED

1993

Rain beat down on the ground, but he remained dry staring up into the lights. He wished more than anything he could feel the water.

"1993?" He looked around. The street looked exactly the same. "1993? But… I… am I…?"

He touched his chest, he felt cold, frozen even.

"I'm dead."

CHAPTER TWO
1999

Summer wrinkled her nose. The place smelled a little funny, like copper and molded popcorn, the busy lobby didn't seem to notice. Families getting snacks, a red headed bartender tossed bottles around happily, a nicely dressed blonde man looked like a stressed out manager, a couple of teenagers on a date, a brunette man ran into the marquee booth holding two large spools of red tickets, a group of young friends pretended they were in the Blair Witch. A cheerleader shoved her boyfriend hard and he stumbled laughing as she pointed her finger up at him feistily, a group of punks cheered a green haired girl on as she fished a stuffed animal out of a claw machine. She hadn't been out in public since she'd moved to Clatter City. It recharged her to see so many excited faces. Movie theaters always had overwhelmingly happy energy, no one was mad to be there.

She pulled on her orange top tossing her blonde hair over her shoulder. Looking over she caught the gaze of one of the multi colored, studded, gang who shoved his friend and they both looked at her smiling. She rolled her eyes and waved before getting her ticket taken and going into theater one. The place was packed, hardly any seats left.

"Should have gotten here earlier." She muttered.

She looked around, wanting to sit anywhere to get out of the way, pausing, she did a double take. A spirit sat in the middle of the crowd, almost like Where's Waldo to spot him at all. Next to him were three empty seats which didn't surprise her, the living avoided the dead subconsciously. How long had he been here? How did he get here? She shuffled past some disgruntled adults whispering,

"Sorry, pardon me."

The ghost didn't acknowledge her, staring at the screen as she sat in a seat down from him. She felt the familiar sting of purposelessness. He was pretty, her age, didn't seem right. She backed down from saying hello in the crowded room, ghosts were unpredictable. One would be friendly, another would try to viciously attack or traumatize you. She shuddered, the specter slowly turned his face to look at her. He looked her up and down, she froze ignoring him staring at the screen. He seemed to sigh, she wondered if ghosts breathed or if things like that were force of habit.

The movie played, people laughed and cried, a few screams. As the room emptied she watched the credits roll by until she was the only one left. She looked over at the man as the lights rose,

"Hey." She whispered leaning over the seat, her hair falling over her shoulder. "Don't freak out."

His dark eyes immediately widened.

"You can… you can… see…"

"Yes." She said smiling gently. "I know you're… do you?"

"Dead?"

Summer sighed in relief. "Sometimes you guys don't, that can be upsetting. I…"

"You shouldn't be able to see me." He rose from his seat floating into the air. "The last two who did, died."

Summer froze, rising, looking up at him. She knew she'd been pulled here.

"Do you want… to tell me about it instead of being all… scary?" She waved her hands around.

A young girl came into the room.

"Miss?" She called out waving. "Did you need any help? I have to shut down the theater."

"Sorry." Summer fake beamed and gathered herself rushing down the steps. She cast a look back, he was gone.

As she left the lobby he popped outside calling out to her from under the marquee,

"Come back tomorrow?"

She turned around and smiled. The people in the long line waiting for tickets from a distressed seeming ticket taker, looked wigged out but smiled back. She nodded and the guy beamed.

"Be careful on… your way home…" She heard him say. "Please." Summer waved back at him walking down the boardwalk into the night.

She strolled along the riverside. The moon slowly inched up the starry sky, a pale tangerine color, not quite full. She stopped in her tracks staring wide eyed into the pitch dark of a small brick tunnel, where a black figure stood. It shuffled slowly towards the light, a mutilated girl with sopping wet dark hair making ink like marks across her face, clad in an outdated windbreaker. She reached out her hands, Summer stepped back. Something wrong and shadowy crawled from the ceiling, dropping behind her dragging her down, she screamed out in pain.

"Ruuunnn!" She shouted and Summer took off, faster than she looked she was back out onto the boardwalk. Smashing into the punks who had been looking at her earlier.

"You okay, Blondie?" The green haired one asked. "Your nose… you're bleeding."

Summer reached up to touch her face, her nose gushing red. One of them pulled out a bandanna and she took it, taking off again, not stopping until she hit home. The last she saw they had been rushing down the stairs saying something about beating up whomever had messed with her.

Waking up the next morning with a jolt she climbed out of her bare white sheeted bed, shuffling through the boxes cluttering her brick and wood apartment. It wasn't the best, but it was cheap. She never stayed in one place for long and ghost hunting didn't pay. Kicking back on an old stool that had come with the place she poured orange juice into a glass. She drank deeply, eyes closed, behind her the tv clicked on.

"Are you ready… to be scared?" A demonic voice growled laughingly from the tv.

Eyes popping open she slowly turned around. She stared wide eyed as the screen bled oozing scarlet all over the floor, tv going white with static. Skeletal hands reached out from the warping glass screen, turning into corpse like arms until a girl's rotted face pushed her way out shrieking, blood flooded the room, she plopped onto the floor spreading out like a screeching spider as the red torrent continued to soak her body.

Summer dropped her orange juice, the glass breaking on the floor mixing with blood as she hopped her kitchen counter sprinting towards the door. The bloody corpse flipped up off the ground onto it's feet gaining speed right behind her, skeletal hands reaching she grabbed at her hair. Summer screamed, opening the door and throwing herself into the wall. She looked back into an empty apartment, the girl gone.

A frail, bald woman opened her door.

"Honey, what the fuck are you doing? You just threw yourself into that wall like you had snakes in your blood."

"There was something... someone in my... apartment."

"Hold on." The woman shut the door and opened it back up with a gun comically big for her body. She strode into her home like muppet, Summer padded cautiously behind her trying to slow her panicked breathing.

"I'm not seeing anyone." She turned around, raising the bald patch where her eyebrow should be. She uncocked her gun. "You need me to keep an eye out for you for a while?"

"I think I'm... I think..." She shook her head in disbelief.

The older woman pulled up a stool.

"I'll stick around."

"Thank you."

Summer shut her door and grabbed a broom sweeping up the glass.

"What's your name, kid?"

"Summer, yours?" She smiled softly at her.

"Detective Rickie Velasquez, retired." She sat her gun down on the table clicking the safety back on. "Towns fuckin' weird." She shook her head, kicking up her slippered feet. Summer grabbed a broom.

"What do you mean?"

"Just weird, 'specially the last few years, but it's always been spooky. Strange things happen, unexplainable. Attracts the odd types. World's one stop, small town, multi-trick pony, freak show."

"Odd types?"

"Ones like you, darlin'. No offense." Rickie tapped her temple. "You got the eye. Don't you?"

"Wish I didn't." Summer leveled. "So what are you?"

"Oh, me?" Rickie smiled, you could tell she'd been a looker. "I'm just trying to survive all of ya."

"What have you seen?"

Rickie laughed, "Too much. On the force thirty years. My sister…" Rickie looked down. "She was like you. What do you call yourselves? Kinetics?"

"That's what I've heard, never meet too many like me..." She winced a little, remembering.

Rickie nodded, "Magda couldn't handle it, did a lot of drugs, died, the whole downward spiral." She made a sucking noise with her mouth, whirlpooling her finger into a sharp thud onto the counter. "The others I've met, they definitely didn't seem as stable as as you."

She gave her a once over.

"How do you handle it?"

Summer looked down.

"Well, I'm fairly strange myself." She shrugged. "An inbetweener."

"You hide it well."

"So do you."

Rickie nodded, "Thank god everyday I wasn't born with it like Magda was. Just sharper than average… intuition we'll call it. You don't get far here without a little edge, especially not as a woman hunting murderers back in the sixties." She whistled. "Clatter City sure needed me, seen some weird crimes go down. You're the one of the few kinetics I've seen without a bottle in their hand or a needle in the arm. What's your poison?"

Summer mimicked Rickie's temple tap.

"Control. It takes a lot to suppress so many of them all of the time. Mental shields developed when I was young. Maybe it's a superpower, I just build walls." She smiled. "Only the strongest ones, the angriest ones…" Her smile faltered like a dying light bulb remembering the blood. "They get through sometimes. Here, I was pulled to Clatter City by…" She shook her head. "Like you said it attracts the odd types."

"You need to be careful. There's been something on the loose, I was tracking it until a few years ago when I got this god damn brain tumor. Doctors said I wouldn't last a year, here I am three and half in. Let's hope I was sticking around for some action."

She felt a trust between the two.

"Thank you."

She readied herself an old band shirt, skirt, boots, bag full of random occult. Saying goodbye to Detective Velasquez the old broad gave her a cookie and a taser.

"Can't ever be too careful." She said, patting her hand. Summer tucked the taser into her back pocket and bit into the cookie.

"Want to have dinner together this week?" Summer said. "I'm a terrible cook."

Velasquez laughed and shooed her on her way agreeing.

Summer found her way to the boardwalk down the road from the theater. It was noon, the once busy street now a ghost town. Walking along she dropped her wallet leaning down to pick it up she heard a groan, she looked around, nothing until a skeleton reached out to grab her hands holding her down to the hot pavement. An innards covered mass of putrid bones crawled from the concrete followed by another, shrieking so loudly Summer felt her insides vibrating. They slipped their sharp fingers into her hair, pulling her face back, peeling up her eyes forcing her to stare at the theater.

Slowly a rotating handheld camera hovered from deep inside the building until it was right in front of her. It spun above her covered in skeleton stickers, the sinister black lens glinted at her as if it were a demonic eye. It pivoted to the wall next to her and projected a moon, the unnatural light from the lens shining the night sky onto her body. The moon revolved to show a skull face in its craters, red weeping down to stain it's glowing body. A torrent of blood poured from the cinema doors like a tidal wave soaking the street. The skeletons shrieked into her ears. Summer cried out.

"Miss? Miss?"

A young man on a bike stopped hopping off, not wanting to touch her his hands waved in front of her face. She snapped out of her reverie, eyes rolling out from the back of her head that was jutted out at an unnatural angle, her arms extended unnaturally. She untensed and wiped her nose, crimson.

"Are you… okay?" He looked like he'd just watched her die.

Summer groaned and pushed herself to her feet.

"I'm, I'm alright."

"Are you sure? Do you need me to call you someone? You looked…" His face twisted.

"No… just uh, de-dehydrated. Thanks, kid." She took off.

Paying to enter, she walked into theater one. Ghost boy in the back, she walked up the stairs of the empty room to sit next to him trying not to show how thrown and tired she was.

"Didn't expect to see you again."

He didn't look at her, but there was something vulnerable there that made Summer sink.

"Told you I would be." She whispered. People always felt uncomfortable if they saw her talking to herself, you knew who was watching even when you thought you were alone.

"The last two girls who were able to see me died so… Can't say you've got long either." He snapped.

"Seen ghosts all my life, haven't keeled over yet."

"So, what, you just hang out with dead people?" He spread his hands open incredulously.

"Sort of, they call us kinetics. Some like me… some different…"

"Ghosts are real?"

"You haven't figured that out?" She laughed.

"Thought maybe it was a space time anomaly."

"Same difference."

The corner of his mouth lifted.

"Vampires, zombies… witches?"

Summer shrugged somberly, "Basically. What's your name?"

"Clive, you?"

"Summer."

"So, you're what… here to resolve my unresolved past and send me to the *beyond,* Summer?"

"I mean… I don't know, I've never seen *beyond*… Don't mind helping you settle your unresolved past. I've done that before I guess."

"How?"

"Told a few people their parents loved them, saved a dog, told the police about… a few murders...".

"Saved a dog?"

"Walking in the woods, dead hiker found me. His friend killed him over his wife, dog had escaped, she was alone in the woods and needed help. Told the police anonymously about the murder, packed up the dog and left town. That was a few years ago." She quieted.

"Didn't go well?"

"You know how it is, you tell them and you're suddenly implicit. Don't stay anywhere too long."

"Was the… dog okay?"

Summer laughed, "She was back to herself in no time, my mom ended up keeping her." She fished out her wallet showing him a Polaroid picture of a hippy looking, frail blonde woman and a small golden retriever.

"She's cute."

"I think she likes the dog more than she liked having a kid." She quirked a not serious smile and shoved the wallet back into her bag.

The theater darkened as multicolored lights flitted into the room.

"Do you think… you were murdered?" Her voice was gentle.

"Is that why people get stuck haunting places?"

Summer shook her head, "Sometimes… mostly it's just trauma. Or maybe…"

"What?"

"Oh, nothing too bleak."

"What, seriously?"

"Maybe some other time."

"Alright." He smiled and dropped it, moving into a cross legged position he sat his hand on his chin and grinned at her seeming to come back more to life and himself the more they talked. "I don't think I was murdered. No one hates me… or hated me. My ex-girlfriend and business partner got married right after but…" He sighed. "I guess I've tried to make my peace with it I mean I'm fucking dead so… what was she going to do, right? I really," He paused looking down at his hands. "I really love her, dude. I want her to be happy."

"I can't say I'd be as calm about it as you…" Summer said sadly. "That sounds like a painful thing to have to watch."

"I've had a lot of time to think about it. The first few years? I was a mess, not easy seeing someone live your dream. Or live at all when you're like… this…"

"How did you…?" Summer made a *chk* sound with her mouth.

"Fire. Up there." He pointed at the projector booth. "I used to run this place. Invested in it with Hunter when the city was considering tearing it down, just… something about the old grind house. She was a piece of work, but we turned her around. Best decision of my life." He made a face and Summer sensed a sad sarcasm. "The girls I've seen though, they were definitely murdered."

"What girls?"

"Emma and Blake. Here one night, dead the next, three years apart. They were the only people to see me this entire time. I don't know how it's connected, I just know they come here before they die."

Summer looked down, "I'm not sure, maybe the veil of the living and dead is thinner before someone is about to pass… I can't explain. I've never heard of anything like that." She shook her head. "There is an extraordinary amount of supernatural energy surrounding the boardwalk though so..." She shuddered thinking of her day.

"Maybe that's why I'm still here. I have to help… them?"

Summer sunk into her seat, eyes wavering. "Where did they die?"

"Emma, down on Riverside. Blake? The paper said her house, I can't read much beyond the front page."

"No leads on who did it?"

"None, the only connection *I've* found is that they come here, see a new Bone Demon movie, then they're dead the next day. It's not like I can tell anyone though."

"Bone Demon?"

"You never watched them? Skeleton guy? Collects bones through brutal demonic homicide, ultimate evil?"

"No I... I mean I've heard of them... Like Jason or Texas Chainsaw Massacre or something?"

"Worse. They scare me way more now at least."

"You really think the movies and the murders are connected? How?"

"I don't know... just don't believe in coincidences. And the next one? Comes out in two days."

She sat back feeling her chest prickle with nerves,

"I've met Emma already I think... Something has been haunting me."

"Haunting?"

"I've been seeing... ghosts. Ones in pain."

"Scary."

"It has been."

"Well, what do you say? Want to solve this shit together?"

He reached out his hand. Summer's heart tightened and they mock shook. Touching him was like touching air coming right out of a freezer.

"We can try."

"Do you know why movie theaters are red?" He asked, jiltedly changing the topic, gesturing to the crimson room.

"Why?"

"Red is the first wavelength of light to disappear when the lights go down."

"Really?"

"Yeah."

"So, what do you do for fun?"

The question caught her off guard.

"What?"

"I don't know, you're the first person I've talked to in years, how do we break the ice here? How much does a polar bear weigh or whatever?"

"For fun… I…?" Summer made a face.

"Do you not have fun?"

"It's just that I'm…"

"What?"

"Kind of a nerd!" Summer threw her hands out defensively.

"A nerd?"

"I just play games really, like Silent Hill. I'm kind of a homebody."

"I miss video games. The last I played was Super Mario."

"How old are you?"

"I was twenty-four when I died, dead for three years then came back as *this* in 1993 and it's been six years of purgatory so... technically I'm thirty now... I guess?"

"Damn, dude."

"What about you? How old are you?"

"Twenty-seven."

"Seriously?"

"Yep."

"Are you actually feeding on the souls out here? You look remarkable."

"Not as good as someone literally preserved in death but alright." She smiled at him.

Clive laughed.

"So what do you do? For fun?" She asked, tilting her head, genuinely curious how he could possibly occupy his time.

"I'm dead so... I watch movies... when they come on it's weird. I don't have any control of what they play so I get what I can get. Funny though you really enjoy it because you only get them the handful of times. I people watch when it's busy. I guess it's the same as before I died I was always at work so... It's my own personal purgatory."

"You seem really… normal… for a ghost."

"You seem really normal for a person who talks to ghosts."

They smiled at one another.

"How far can you go from the theater?"

"Not too far. When I do I'm just," He made a sucking noise with his mouth, "right back to the marquee.The whooshing is a little disorienting so I don't mess with it a lot."

"What if I could change that?"

His eyes went wide, "What do you mean?"

"I can tether us so we can walk around together."

"Why would you do that for me?"

"I'm on a self destructive streak I guess." She shrugged. "Really, just seems the right thing to figure out who's hurting these girls before they get someone else. It'll take some work to figure out the tether." Summer cringed. "I've never really done it before."

"What do you mean?"

"I'll see you tonight around four am, meet you outside?"

"Sure, I..."

"I'll see you later." Summer stood up to go, he hovered next to her mock walking down the seats like they were steps.

"What're you going to do?" He jumped and flowed onto his back hands behind his head, gliding as if he was in zero gravity. "Nothing unsafe I hope."

"Of course not."

"You're lying."

Summer hid a smile as she pushed the doors to enter the lobby. They swung back through him as he followed her.

"Why won't you tell me what you're going to do?"

"The less you know the better." She mumbled waving to the pretty bartender on her way out. He paused outside under the marquee as she walked out of his reach.

"Be careful!" He shouted urgently. "You're the only person I've talked to in six years, dude! Seriously!" Summer paused before looking over her shoulder, eyes crinkling into mock confidence and nodded.

Midnight, the moon rose white above her. Stones in the cemetery shone against the wet black of the grass. She found her way to a tombstone carved into a marquee.

HERE LIES CLIVE
1969-1990
THE END

"Only you, Clive." She muttered with a tilt of her mouth, she pulled a marker out of her pocket and placed a small question mark, making it,

She laughed and started digging into the years undisturbed ground.

She couldn't believe she was doing this, not grave robbing, she'd dug up a few bodies in her twenty-seven years but she'd never gone as far to do a soul tie. Was she sure she wanted to? She paused leaning on her shovel huffing. Down in the grave past her head.

"They really weren't fucking around when they said six feet deep."

She kept going til her shovel hit wood, something nervous rang through her at the thought of actually having to open the casket. She didn't want to see him like that. She heard a soft thump behind her and slowly turned, spindly skeleton arms were shoving their way out of the soft dirt behind her followed by two more on either side. Summer suppressed a scream as the mound of bones thudded in front of her slowly rising, dirt falling in clumps. In its hand a spine shaped knife. It ran at her stabbing her multiple times.

Summer gurgled as it passed the knife to the second now standing behind her. It ripped back her hair cutting open her throat, the third grabbed her by the neck levitating her into the air where her legs kicked and reached for footing as she choked. Blood rained down from the sky like a storm, the red filling the grave like a pool.

The skeleton dropped her, she fell sinking through the thickness like an anchor landing in the casket where it slammed shut. Summer regained consciousness inside of the closed coffin and screamed pounding on the door, it easily popped open and she scrambled out into the empty grave touching her unhurt skin, tears mixing with dirt.

"Fucking… skeletons!!" She shouted.

Kicking the dirt wall falling to her knees. She hit her head with her fist where her eye was and repressed a cornered scream. She took a moment trying to recapture her breath until her head did a double take back to Clive's coffin. The body was… gone. She ripped it open and searched, for anything there had to be some piece of him… in the corner of the casket sat a small bag. Summer touched her dirty hand to her mouth and tried not to throw up.

"Not the baaaag." She whined.

She reached over and lugged it out, not as heavy as she imagined it must have been had it been fresh, the insides had the thick consistency of play dough, once liquid. She tossed it to the top, pulling her way up and out of the grave. Out of breath she wiped her head breathing heavily until it caught in her chest from terror. In the darkness just beyond her sight a horned skeleton stood, small red light shining from the black, Summer screamed and fell back.

"Who's out there!" She heard a man holler. "You weirdo goth kids better not be getting fresh with them graves!"

Summer looked around, the skeleton was gone. Checking her mud covered appearance, and dodging the searching flashlight beam cutting the safety of darkness she grabbed the organ bag and ran.

Dragging her way into her apartment she threw the bag onto the ground. Whipping her clothes off, shuddering as a beetle fell out of her bra, running for the shower. Blood and dirt washed down the drain. She looked in the mirror, marks reddened around her neck where she'd been lifted into the air. The cotton sleep shirt felt like a relief on her skin.

Checking the clock she saw it was nearly midnight. She grabbed multiple candles from a box labeled, "**PARANORMAL**." She pulled out an old handwritten book and flipped through finding a winding symbol. She choked and sputtered in disgust as she dipped her hand into the gummy substance that was Clive's liquified organs. She drew the large circular symbol gagging and holding her breath as she drew the same symbol on her third eye, before plopping the organ bag into the middle of the circle.

Her heart leapt out of her chest as she started to light the candles murmuring the words from the book,

"*NORTH TO SOUTH*
EAST TO WEST
WE ARE BOUND."

When she lit the last the blood lit up like a beacon. All at once she was surrounded by demonic skeletons looking down on her with black sockets, permanent grins. Grabbing for her hair, eyes, skin, the mob shredded her body, ripping fistfuls and pulling her open as the contents of her stomach spilled onto the floor, their fingers filled her jaw and she gurgled out in agony. They disappeared, Clive in the middle of the circle standing on his organ sack looking sick. He stumbled to the corner of her apartment and threw up plasma onto the ground. Summer's eyes rolled into the back of her head and she passed out forwards in the middle of the symbol, blood smearing onto her face, candles wooshing out.

She groaned, light hitting her closed eyelids. She moved around grunting before opening her eyes to see bright green ones. She yelped and Clive peered at her as she slowly sat up moaning like a zombie.

"It's… it's a Clive!" She groaned, throwing her arms out in triumph.

"You have something on your face." He grimaced.

Summer touched the thick substance and brought it down to look at.

"Oh god I'm going to be sick." She got up running to the bathroom throwing up.

"What is it?" He called after her.

"It's… you!" She yelled back.

She heard him laugh, "That's what she said."

Summer finished puking and started washing the foul smelling substance off of her face.

"That's not fucking funny." She snapped, popping her head out of the bathroom, face totally covered in suds. Clive fell back levitating in the air laughing uncontrollably.

"What the hell do you mean it's me?" He said trying to regain composure.

"I dug up your grave last night." She said coming out still scrubbing her face but with new soap, more soap.

"Words every man wants to hear."

Summer popped an irritated eyebrow at him and rinsed her face multiple times before washing it again.

"Where are we even? Your apartment?" He gestured to her video games scattered all over the floor. "You weren't kidding about being an absolute nerd, you nerd! Is this a DnD book? Did no one ever tell you, you're hot or what's going on right now?"

"Oh, shut up! I'm allowed to like things!"

He popped over and peaked into the bathroom where she was rinsing her face.

"No, seriously, it's cool. You seem cool."

"Can I have a little privacy please?"

He popped out back next to the window peering outside, "I mean what is even happening right now?"

"I did a… soul tie." Summer plopped her face into a fluffy towel.

"Does that mean we're… dating?"

"No, we are solving murders, you ass."

"Whatever." He laughed and kicked at the ground. "I was just kidding."

"Where I go, you can go. You can also go back to the theatre anytime you want. You just have to think about it and you'll be there."

"Wow, seriously? So you're, what, like a soul taxi cab?"

"A way to put it, yeah."

"You had to dig up my body for that? I can't believe you went through all that trouble. Thank you, Summer…"

"Yeah about your body… it's sort of… gone…"

Clive looked incredulous.

"Gone?"

"Missing, stolen, pilfered, misplaced, finito. Ordinarily I'd just need you know maybe a finger or something but your body was gone… like taken, removed, bodynapped. I guess it's lucky you died in a fire because your body was so destroyed they didn't do an open casket and left your organ bag just out next to your feet."

"Organ bag?"

"They scoop you out before burying you. Usually that bag would be inside of your body but lucky for us they were lazy."

"Oh, well that's certainly comforting." He said sarcastically. "So who took me?"

Summer shrugged.

"I'm not sure but it's to the point this is getting a little… wacky. You don't want the wrong someone to have your body after death… are you sure you didn't have any enemies?"

"No, I'm fucking awesome?"

Summer laughed tossing her towel into her hamper.

"Remains to be seen."

"Was that supposed to be a joke?"

"What? I, no." She laughed again and went to her fridge chugging juice right from the carton.

"Well, I mean…" He gestured to the bag and she spit orange.

"Fucking stop."

"I mean… I don't know my partner was pretty quick to marry my ex girlfriend, but they're good people they wouldn't… you know."

"You don't know about anyone." Summer said very seriously looking into his eyes. "Anyone."

"You think we should check them out?"

"It's a lead…"

"That feels lame, but okay. Do we have a plan on how to… figure out what's been… going on? You *really* think someone killed me?"

"They took your body is all I really know…" She popped the fridge closed. "Like you were talking about yesterday with the girls coming to the theater and seeing you before being hurt, can't believe in coincidences. Let's get looking for it."

"Where do we start?"

"At Riverside, where Emma was murdered." Summer closed her eyes where Clive couldn't see. The visions were taking their toll on her but having him there, she felt better.

They walked down the river path, it had been slow going, Clive was like a puppy that hadn't been out of the house in months. He had to stop and look at pretty much everything. Summer didn't blame him, his enthusiasm was infectious.

"I'm outside!!!!" He yelled jumping and clicking his heels together. He did an air somersault, floating his way on his back to Mary.

"Dude, I can't thank you enough, it's so weird to take a walk down the street I feel like I just got out of jail."

"I'm glad you're enjoying yourself." Summer paused staring where she had been chased last night. "Don't thank me yet I don't know what I'm getting into."

"Where should we start?"

Summer pointed to the tunnel.

"In there."

She walked forward making a face.

"What's wrong? You look scared."

"Just not sure what we are about to see here."

"I have your back."

Summer looked at him and genuinely smiled.

"Thank you."

Into the shadow of the tunnel they walked Summer's eyes on the ceiling where she'd seen the dark figure crawl from two days before, slowly she moved her vision in a circle settling on the middle of the tunnel floor. Shakingly she walked forward the air getting colder with each step. The light sucked out of the tunnel until a crimson flash glowed beneath her feet, a symbol she'd seen somewhere in long forgotten nightmares. The air went red, Clive froze next to her, and Summer fell to her knees.

CHAPTER THREE
1993

Emma sat in the theater Bone Demon Two: The Summoning had just come out. She tossed her long black hair over her shoulder, hairsprayed and crimped to high heaven. Her date had stood her up. She sunk into her seat pouting, sucking soda through a straw. Was she not pretty? She felt like she was really pretty. So why were boys always acting like such losers?

She crossed her long legs clad in light purple tights. Was it her outfit? Had he seen her and just ran? Did people not want to make out anymore? Rachel said this guy was cool.

A brunette girl on the screen screamed running from the killer. Frustration hit her and she got up heading for the doors. The only other person in the audience was some weird looking guy in a Canadian tuxedo. He stared at her wide eyed as she left, he kept staring so she made a face at him and his mouth popped open. He said something but she couldn't hear over the girl dying in the movie. Pushing through the double doors she walked out through the lobby, throwing her soda away she waved to the friendly blue haired barkeep. She stood underneath the marquee and pulled some spearmint gum out of her bag. Next to her an abnormally attractive, blonde man was on the payphone.

"Look, Gwen, I want to come home but… I *know* what day it is, okay? I can't, I just can't right now."

You could hear a feminine voice shout from the earpiece,

"But Hunter I really need…"

He looked over at her and she smiled automatically. He looked her up and down gazing at her and she slowly turned to walk down the boardwalk, when she looked over her shoulder he was still looking at her smiling a little before going back to arguing with the phone. She rolled her eyes, but grinned. Couldn't be mad about some much needed validation after a shitty night.

She padded her way along the sidewalk pushing her hands into her breaker jacket pockets, taking a turn she traipsed down the stairs to the river path. Pausing by the twinkling water she watched an unusually red moon rise.

"Woah. Pretty." She leaned against the rail.

She heard something behind her and turned, seeing nothing. Frowning, she continued down the path pausing before going into the darkly lit tunnel. It was only twenty feet across, but it was enough darkness to wig her out. She stepped forward seeing something pale painted onto the ground she couldn't make out it's shape. Hearing a scuttle she spun on her heel. A flash of something white before it turned, just out of the light of the street lamp.

"Hello?" She said, pissed off already. A red light beamed from the dark. "What the hell." The street light glinted against something glass. She took a couple of steps forward squinting into the black, "What is… what is that…?" On the fringe of darkness a shape… It stepped forward, a skeleton painted onto a black suit that bled into the night as an optical illusion. Topped with a grinning skull mask sprouting horns made of bone. The creature was holding a video camera up to his blackened eyepiece.

"This is the part where you run." He gravelled.

Emma screamed and took off, the skeleton set the camera down, chasing her pulling a white knife made of a human spine from his suit. He tackled her, crawling up her struggling body. In the viewfinder of the camcorder, he stabbed her hundreds of times.

Clive lay in the air on his back watching the sunrise through the doors, thinking about the raven haired girl from a few nights before. Had she seen him? Really? No one had noticed him in the six months he'd been back. Floating down next to a paper cut out of Morticia Addams he sighed.

"Do you think she saw me, Mortie? She made a face…" He laughed remembering how cute it had been. "I probably freaked her out."

The closest anyone had been to seeing him was when he'd gotten so mad about them not cleaning the popcorn machine he accidentally stomped the plug out of the wall, the only thing he'd touched in the six months he'd been back. Scared Marina out of her socks.

A blue haired girl came to unlock the doors.

"Think of the devil."

Walking in, her face was perturbed. She threw down a newspaper the headline read,

"Riverside Murder"

-

The picture underneath the girl from the other night. Clive tried to hit the counter in anger but his hand went right through. He shouted out in frustration and Marina turned around.

"Hello?" She said, but she looked right through him.

CHAPTER FOUR
1999

"Summer. Summer. Summer. Seriously, wake up. Wake up please. Dude, Sum…"

Her eyes popped open and she breathed in, scrambling backwards. She got up running out of the tunnel into the sunshine blood spilling from her nose. Clive behind her.

"Hey, dude, slow down you just… man, your face was that a seizure? You really scared me."

She didn't say anything huffing her way back home. In her apartment she went to her fridge pulling out a carton of orange juice, chugging it, getting blood on the cardboard. Grabbing a soft towel she tenderly cleaned herself up with cool water.

"Dude, will you say something? You run mega fast, guy. You're like the terminator, fuck." Floating up he sat on the counter looking at her. Her blonde hair stuck to her neck and her chest fluttered as she breathed heavily. He wanted to reach out and touch her, comfort her and he couldn't.

Summer grabbed her bloody orange juice pushing herself up onto the counter opposite him. She took a breath, a drink and paused.

"I saw… I saw the… I felt…" She shook her head and explained to him what had transpired. "It was like a dream. I saw it all from the outside, even parts of what happened with you." She finished.

"He was dressed like the Bone Collector, really?"

"Yeah, but he had horns like… what I saw when we tethered. And… He was… he fucking filmed it."

"You're joking."

"No."

Sitting in silence the fan whirred behind them.

"Movie night?" She said hopping down from the counter.

Clive shuddered having seen all of the Bone Demons multiple times, they seemed wrong now.

"What I'm best at." He said, forcing a smile for her.

Finding themselves at the video rental shack, Summer immediately bought some candy shoving it into her mouth.

"Why do you eat so much sugar?"

"Just low energy lately, a lot of nose bleeds." She muttered. "Why being judgmental?"

"Not judgmental, just concerned. Maybe you should eat some iron or…"

"Okay, Dad." She said browsing through the horror section.

"Well it's not like anyone can survive on just licorice and orange juice, butthead."

"Found it." She pulled out a stack of three Bone Demon movies, covers made up of blood and bones. One was just a skull which she held up to her face and made a snarfelling sound with her throat.

"Not funny, dude."

They checked out and went back to Summer's apartment where she ordered a pizza and sat legs crossed on thet floor. Clive floated behind her laying on her couch, they zipped through the first movie to the second.

"I miss pizza." He said, staring longingly at the pepperonis.

"It's overrated." She said.

"Thank you for lying."

He reached down and touched her head as if ruffling her hair but all she felt was cool air. She looked back at him smiling before returning her attention to the Skeleton man as he raised a knife made of a human spine and bone into the air.

"Hey did you see that?"

"See what?" She rewound to the part where the Collector had a young girl on a symbol.

"That… there… I've seen that before… I think that's the same one from Riverside even…" She threw her pizza down and went to wash her hands before pulling out her small old book from the night prior. "That's a… oh my god…"

"What?"

"That's a *real* summoning circle… how could they… where did they get that?"

"With the internet now…"

"Oh no…" She put her head in her hands.

"What do you mean, summoning… what?"

"There's a lot of good in the world, Clive. So there has to be a lot of bad too… that… whatever the person who mimicked these movies if they drew that… they brought out something really nasty, a demon is how I would describe it."

"You mean someone has been copying the movies and accidentally summoned something real?"

"Clutter City attracts all kinds of types, maybe someone had kinetic energy and accidentally?"

"If it was an accident at all…"

"Right."

"Where do we go from here?"

"I guess we have to go check out the site where the other girl was murdered, Blake?" Summer yawned, leaning her head back, she could feel Clive's cold leg.

"You need some rest."

"No I don't." She said, rubbing her eyes and ugly yawning again. "We have to finish the last movie."

"I think we found out all we really need."

"Maybe." Summer slowly lay onto the floor stretching out like a cat.

"You're not going to get into your bed?" He laughed.

"Too faaaarrrr…" She groaned, but really she didn't want to sleep by herself.

"Okay." He moved onto his side looking down at her. "This is the most fun I've had in a long time… despite… you know… all of the death."

Her form jiggled, laughing and he couldn't keep the smile off his face either.

"Honestly… me too. I don't… make a lot of friends doing what I do."

"Seems to me you're the kind that makes friends everywhere you go."

Summer's nose twitched and her brow furrowed.

"Then maybe that's the problem, always giving too much of yourself to others."

"Good people always seem to."

She rolled over and he could see she was trying not to cry.

"It's tough."

"I'm sure a lot of people really appreciate… how you help them. I know I do…"

She reached up and touched his hand.

"I'm glad you're here."

She fell asleep like that.

  The next day they found themselves in front of Blake's old house. A small red for sale sign sat in a bunch of overgrown weeds. Glass was broken out, 666, Gay Satanist, The Devil Was Here, various vulgar body parts, and a bunch of pentagrams were spray painted half hazardously adding insult to injury to the sad looking house.

"Looks like they were never able to sell the place..." She said.

"Can't imagine, "Ritualistic Murder" is, uh, a great selling point."

In the house a shadowy figure passed by the window.

"Did you see that?"

"Yeah... is someone, was that a ghost?"

"You can't see ghosts..."

"Yeah, but..."

"I mean I'm dead can't the dead see the other dead? Isn't being close to death the key, dying in a fire feels pretty close."

"No, unless you're kinetic before you die you can't. You've never seen anyone else have you?"

"I... shadows kind of."

"Probably picking up on small stuff but the afterlife isn't like a club where you can just chill with Kurt Cobain."

"Pretty bleak. And if you died?"

"Not sure… haven't done that yet. Maybe I can still see people… Like I said my type is few and far between. You don't meet a lot of us dead or alive. The ones that do have it often go crazy after puberty. Just too much for them to handle, can't say their ghosts would be great company."

"So someone is in the house?"

"I think… that was… a spirit."

"You just said I couldn't see them."

"Rethinking it and adding in the soul tie maybe… maybe you're picking up on more."

Clive shuddered, "Ghosts creep me out."

Summer nodded, "Ironic, but understandable. This is not going to be pleasant."

"It's October may as well kick it off with a haunted house." Clive sighed. "I don't have much to be scared of, I'm already dead but you I mean… you need to be careful in here."

"Still plenty to fear when you're dead, but point taken."

"What do you mean?" Clive panicked but she was already moving towards the blue chipping painted doors. "Can't just leave a dude hanging like that…" He grumbled rushing behind her.

She turned the knob and the door popped open, creaking it's way slowly revealing a dirty and dusty kitchen. Clive peeked over her shoulder.

"Dude, do you have like… a gun?"

"You can't shoot a ghost."

"I meant if there's a person in here."

Summer pulled out the taser Detective Velasquez had given her and zapped it.

"I guess that works."

The pale green door to the basement flung open smacking against the wall making both of them jump.

"You want me to go first?" He said floating into the house peering into the darkness of the basement. "I don't… I don't see anything."

Summer creeped in behind him, not really wanting to leave the small patch of light that meant she could still run out of the door at a moment's notice.

Summer looked to the living room. Two skeletons holding hands stood in the dingy dark, their grinning faces seemed to warp and their jaws popped open as blood gushed forth from their eye sockets covering their white bodies. Summer looked away, closing her eyes and counting to three.

"Are you okay?" When she opened them Clive was close to her face looking concerned.

"I'm… let's just get this over with."

She stepped past him looking into the darkness, she flipped the switch, nothing. Pulling a flashlight out of her bag she shon it down the stairs. Cobwebs and brown mortar but that was it. The concrete ground looked dirty and blackened. Something foul resonated from deep in the pit.

Clive moved past her,

"Let me take the lead fair lady." He guffawed his slightly glowing form floating down into the darkness. Summer slowly followed. At the bottom of the stairs she saw Clive standing in the corner, back to her looking at something.

"What… what is it." She said and coming up behind him and gasping. Old dried maroon blood was everywhere, a large demonic symbol etched into the ground, the skull of a rotted animal, old candles settled in dusty, waxed, permanent fixtures having been apart of something very wrong. She shone the flashlight behind her and up to the ceiling. How was there so much dried blood?

She heard something and they both turned as the door from upstairs slammed shut, in the corner a red light turned on, a skeleton figure rushed from the darkness and Summer fell to her knees screaming.

CHAPTER FIVE
1996

•CINEMA•
ADMIT ONE

Blake looked down at her ticket, shaking the back of her dark pixie cut with her many silver ringed hand. Something about going inside any place made her want to turn around and go back home instead. She hadn't left the house in so long even her dog thought she was a loser. Her mom called her ten times a day,

"Move on! She was no good for you! Get a new girlfriend! It's the 90s, do whatever you want!"

To the dismay of her wallowing misanthropy, everyone had been talking about how good was and she was determined to see it before a trailer ruined it for her. They showed every single plot point, in detail, hundreds of times a day on tv. Avoiding spoilers was like dodging bullets. They used to come to The Silver Theatre often before she and Cora broken up, now she avoided it like the plague. Her long time friend, bartender of the silver cinema, Marina, had invited her out. She figured the coast was clear.

Going inside the look on Marina's face made the smile on hers wither.

"Blake I tried to call but you already left the house…" She muttered.

Cora walked out of theatre one holding hands with a red head she assumed was Elena. She stopped abruptly, seeing Blake immediately looking guilty.

"Hey…" She said looking from Elena to her.

Blake didn't respond walking up to the bar.

"Can I have a beer?"

"Blake, please…"

"Cora." She replied, frustrated. "You've done enough. Can you just go?"

Cora had the audacity to look hurt.

"I don't want it to be like this, we can be friends…"

"I'm not interested in your friendship. Can I see a movie in peace or is that too much?"

"Cora, let's go." Elena said, pulling her hand. Blake couldn't help but glare at the tall pretty girl as she took the person she thought she'd spend the rest of her life with out the door.

"I don't like to take sides…" Marina said, looking guilty. "But she's kind of a bitch." She popped the top on the beer and slid it down the wooden bar into Blake's hand.

"Tell me about it. Can you believe she made me buy that house? And just dipped? She's tripping we can be friends. Yeah, fifty thousand dollar in debt friends." Blake took a long swig downing half her beer.

"It is a pretty cool house at least." Marina smiled.

"If I can afford to even stay in it."

"Is it that bad?" Marina leaned onto the bar looking sad.

Blake sighed, "I'll be working pretty much everyday for the next four years but…" Blake shook her head. "At least it'll be mine." She chugged the rest of the beer and tossed it into the trash. "Can I have another one, or make that two since I'm going to be there a while?"

"Yeah for sure, and don't worry these are on me. I really did try to call you. Sorry you had to see that."

Blake slapped twenty onto the counter, "Don't worry about it, Marina. This movie better not suck though."

An attractive blonde man came down the steps from the projector rooms.

"Oh, don't fear," He grinned. "It's killer." He walked over to the taps pulling out a keg, sliding a new heavy one into its place without effort.

"Nice to see you back, Blake." He grunted. "I haven't seen you around in a while." He smiled standing, she didn't talk to Hunter much but she knew he owned the place.

"Nice to see you too, dude." She saluted him. "Better go don't want to miss the new trailer reel."

Cradling her beers to her chest like babies she walked into theater one. Adrenaline and alcohol were the only things preventing her from crying. She'd spent months avoiding that sight, but at least it was here and not the grocery store in the middle of the night when she looked like a bum.

She plopped down near the top of the empty theatre. Climbing those black stairs into the red void of seats was akin to Mount Everest. She propped her feet up on the back of the seat and immediately heard a loud grunt of frustration. She looked around, not seeing anyone, before up to the projector booth raising an eyebrow.

"Really that stiff about the seats?"

She clunked her feet onto the sticky ground, the lights lowered. Weird animated Ferris wheel advertisement, trailer, trailer, dancing popcorn cartoons, go to the bathroom now warnings, smother your children into silence or be removed, more trailers. She waterfalled beer into her mouth. One person entered sitting at the front, a dark shape against the light tossing popcorn into their mouth.

BONE DEMON THREE: THE SACRIFICE

Popped onto the screen along with the signature demon skull mask. She quirked a smile, why did this weird shit always make her feel better?

"Two beers? She must be having a bad night."

She heard someone whisper. Blake stood up and looked behind her, no one. She looked up towards the projector booth, filtering light through a square.

"Judgemental much?" She said.

"Shhhh!" She heard from the front. The man had turned around, now joined by a shadowy woman.

"Tell me to sh." She grumbled, settling into her seat defiantly putting her feet back up.

She chugged the rest of her beer with unashamed gusto. The franchise's ever changing final girl came onto screen. This one wasn't like previous heroines, with their chestnut hair and doe eyes. She had dark hair, olive skin, tomboyish qualities that you didn't get to see on screen often. In Blake's stupor she attached instantly. Quieting she tucked her knees into her chest, hugging them, staring at the screen like a moth would a flame.

"They found her body." A man said to the final girl.

"I told you he was back."

"I told you he was back." Blake heard a voice next to her mimic the dialogue.

She looked over and jumped to see a dark haired man in a Canadian tuxedo a seat down from her. He was watching the screen. How he had gotten there without her seeing she had no idea.

"We have to stop him before he raises Osseous."

"We have to stop him before he raises Osseous."

"How, Saige? He possesses the dagger of reincarnation…"

"How, Saige? He possesses the dagger of reincarnation…"

"We steal it back."

"We steal it back."

"Dude, can you stop?" She whispered. His head snapped over to hers so fast she moved back a little. "Sorry, you're just being kind of loud. How many times have you seen this even?"

He looked from the screen to her, to the screen, to her.

"You can… can you see me?"

"I…" Blake looked around incredulously. "Yes… Jack Griffin, I can see you."

The guy smiled so big Blake felt creeped out and disarmed at the same time. She took a swig of her beer and in the moment she raised it and put it back down his expression had twisted.

"You… you have to be careful." He said and moved a seat closer to her. "You have to… you could please be careful. You shouldn't be able to see me."

"Ooo..Kay?" Blake said, raising an eyebrow while taking another drink.

"Stop… *drinking,* you're not safe."

"What?"

"When people see me I don't think… I mean I'm dead… you have to be careful." The guy reached out to grab her and Blake dodged, he barely grazed her but he was freezing cold.

"Dude… what the hell?"

"Miss, can you please be quiet?" The man from the front yelled.

"Me… what about him?"

"Listen to me!" The dark haired guy shouted moving towards her.

Blake got up and ran out of the theater.

"Marina! Dude…"

"Oh my god, what?" Startled Marina hopped from her perch on a stool.

"There's some weird guy in there like in a Canadian tuxedo he's saying…? He's dead? I don't know."

"What?" Marina froze looking scared.

"Are you… but no one… does he have dark hair and a shirt that says horror?"

"Yeah?"

Marina backed away from her, quieting. Hunter came out of the office looking from Marina to Blake.

"Is there something wrong?"

"Hunter, she saw Clive."

He froze.

"There's just some guy in a Canadian tuxedo in there saying something about how he's dead? I don't know…"

"Is this your idea of a joke?" He said suddenly angry. "It's not fucking funny, Marina. We talked about bringing up these *ridiculous* ghost stories."

"You know what, Hunter? I quit. I'm not fucking… fuck this…the place is haunted. You're crazy, things have been going on for the last six years and I've been telling you it's getting weirder. The popcorn machine, the light bulbs, just the other day I heard him laughing in an empty theater and someone screaming!"

"Get out!" Hunter yelled. "Just get out!"

Marina teared up, grabbing her things.

"Don't worry, I'm leaving!"

A beautiful, dark skinned,l raven haired woman stepped out of the office.

"Hunter what's going on? Why is Marina upset?"

Marina stormed out and Blake stood there stunned.

"It's nothing, Gwen. Don't worry about it."

"I'm sorry dude I just thought… it was a weird guy on drugs… I? Sorry…" She left, as she was going she saw Hunter behind her in the reflective glass glaring after her.

"Marina!" Blake ran outside, the bright lights of the theater fading out as she chased her down the street.

"What the hell, man?" She huffed as put the key into her passenger side, lumbering over her stick shift to the driver's seat. Blake put her hands on her knees, the booze were starting to really hit her system.

"Ugh…" She said.

"You need a ride?" Marina said defeatedly from the car.

"Probably for the best." Blake clunked into the passenger seat and dragged the heavy door shut with a slam.

"I knew I shouldn't have given you that many beers."

"It's not like I expected to be jostling around on a carbonated stomach." She groaned. "What the fuck even was that?"

"Look, sorry, there's been something really weird going on for a while."

"What do you mean? You guys sound…." She widened her eyes and tensed her hands next to her eyes.

"The place is… it's fucking haunted… Clive was one of the owners six years ago, before you and Cora started coming around. He got trapped in theater one's projection room during a fire, burned to death."

"I remember hearing something about that." She squinted like if would help her recall.

"He's been… haunting or *something* the place the last few years, not sure what's going on maybe he's mad Hunter married Gwen. I just know that I have seen some weird shit and I'm *not* fucking crazy. I mean you saw him tonight!"

"I saw a weird guy… I mean…." She shrugged.

"It's not even just that, remember the Riverside killer from last year?"

"Oh man… that got that girl? Yeah…"

"I don't know, she was in right before and I'm… I'm getting some real bad vibes, you get it?"

"No… not really. Some guy was freaking out in the theater, now it's ghosts and riverside murderers?" Blake felt a little woozy.

"Something isn't right. It's just been off there, the energy, everything. I've been having nightmares."

"What about?"

"You're going to think I'm crazy…"

Blake tried hard not to make a face, her first night out was going so well she would probably never leave the house again.

"It's about the… the Bone Demon movies and… sometimes Clive, this girl, I don't know. It's really weird. I…" She looked from Blake back to the road sounding unsure. "I've only had repetitive dreams about things, like… that… come true? Sort of? Like me winning the spelling bee or my mom getting pregnant with my sister, even me getting the job at the theatre, my dad I knew when he had cancer and… So… it's been kind of unsettling."

"So you think you're what… a seer or something?" Blake tried to keep the panic from her face, she bit her lip, how was this going so south?

"I know how it sounds, I'm not trying to be like that. I think sometimes our minds pick up on small hints and clues that we don't fully understand and then they manifest themselves or something. So whatever it is I'm picking up on here, Blake?" Marina made eye contact with her. "It was enough to make me quit tonight. No one went into that theater wearing that… no one. It was Clive."

"Yeah well I wouldn't want to work with a ghost." Blake sighed and slid down her seat. "Sorry about your job, dude."

"Mm, time for a change. No one should work in the same job for six years. I just liked the people I think. Kind of sad I didn't think it would end like that. All the other bartenders got a party." She smiled sadly.

They drove the rest of the way in silence as tunes softly played over the radio.

Pulling up to her house Blake couldn't get out of the car fast enough.

"Thanks for the ride, girl." She said leaning down to the window.

"Anytime." Marina looked a little wide eyed for some reason. "I'll watch you go inside, okay?"

Blake nodded, turning and walking through her picket fence, up her stairs. She slid her key into the lock waving behind her. Marina's blue hair glowed in the street lamp, she waved back. She drove off as Blake walked inside.

Standing in her kitchen she locked the door, resting her forehead against the frame.

"That suuuuuuuucked." She whispered and thunked her head against the wood. "Literally worst case scenario." She emphasized each word with a thunk of her head.

She heard a whimper from her living room.

"Sandra?" She called out to her dog, who usually greeted her immediately when she opened the door. She walked into her living room. "Sandra, babe, where are you?" The tv was on but it was dark. She flipped on the light. Nothing. She walked into the bedroom, frowning. "Sandra?" Her voice was a little panicked. She turned the lights on, thinking she'd be on the bed, nothing. She hit the bathroom, ripping back the curtain. No sign of her dog. She walked around checking the windows, the spare bedroom. Nothing. Full blown fear set in. "Sandra, here girl?"

She traced her thoughts back to when she'd left, her golden brown spotted face smiling as she shut the door. She was positive she'd heard her... another whimper. Blake looked down, it was coming up from a vent from the basement.

She ran to the door flinging it open and flipping the light switch, it didn't work. It was dark, she called out for her dog again, no answer. Slowly she made her way down the stairs feeling along the wall. Touching down on the bottom step she rounded the corner to see a candle lit in the furthest corner of the room. Her heart stopped. She crept along the wall towards the flickering light as she got closer she cried out. Sandra's dismembered head was splayed open the candle shoved into her mouth, next to a giant weaved symbol carved into the floor.

Behind her a bright light clicked on, she turned around like a deer in the headlights. A man all in black with his back to the corner turned around showing a skeleton suit and mask tipped with horns, in his hand a yellowed white, misshapen, knife with what looked like a spine for a hilt. Blake screamed and went to kick him but he grabbed her full leg throwing her down onto the symbol.

He climbed on top of her pinning her down with his knees, he was impossibly strong. She tried to punch him and he grabbed her hands pushing both her wrists back and breaking them nearly tearing them completely. Blake wailed until he took his knife cutting under her chin, making her go silent, choking. He pulled something from her throat, a U shaped bone.

"Now. You can't scream." He raised up the knife with both hands, about to plunge it into her chest when they heard a loud knock upstairs.

"Blake!" She heard a woman yell. "Hey Blake! It's Marina!!" She heard the door open. "Hey Blake! I'm sorry I know I'm bothering you I just… I had a bad… feel…"

Marina saw the basement door, to her it was bright red. Her heart stopped in her chest. She grabbed a poker from next to the fireplace. She'd seen this door before, somewhere.

"Blake!" She cried out. No answer. She creeped around the basement staring into the black with wide eyes, she felt something cruel coming from the dark. She picked up the phone from the wall, no dial tone. Taking a frustrated breath she called out, "Blake, send me any kind of sign here!"

She reached out a hand as soon as it hit the doorway air it felt searingly hot. She ripped it back touching her fingers to her mouth. Shakingly she reached out and pushed her hand through, as it did it rapidly decayed, skin falling off and turning to bone. She blinked, a split second hallucination, and it was back to normal. She stepped back from the swirling darkness, until she heard Blake's voice echo distortedly from below.

"…here… here… here…"

Marina cursed under her breath slowly descending the stairs, back to the wall, poker ready to strike. Two skeleton hands reached from between the stairs tripping her, she stumbled falling into the wall bouncing back quickly. A dark shape ran at her punching the wall sending brick along the ground. Marina spun and struck out, a horned skull face snapped up to look at her grabbing the poker mid swing.

He laughed a deep rumbling sound, slowly rising he ripped the metal from her grasp bending it in front of her. Eyes wide, Marina fell stumbling backwards into something warm. Looking down Marina found she was in the middle of a carved symbol filled with blood spilling from Blake's body. Blake's panicked eyes fluttered as she took a last shuddered breath and died.

"No… no, no, no…"

Looking up the skeleton approached, camera in hand shining a light down on her, something sharp in his fist.

"Mmm.." Said a familiar voice. "Kinetic blood… powerful. You know we have a special bone, here." He tapped the back of his neck with the knife. "And part of the brain here." He tapped his forehead. "That's what allows us to pick up on the wavelengths of the dead. Do more than the average person."

"You can't be…"

"It's always the ones you least expect."

He pointed the knife like a wand and her body raised into the air, she grabbed at her throat her toes kicking out for something to stand on. He set the camera into a tripod and came down on her with the bone blade. Her blood sprayed out, overflowing the divets of the glowing glyph as he cut out the parts of her that gave her the sight. He threw his head back holding up a spiral like bone in front of Marina's levitating corpse laughing inhumanly.

Clive lay above the middle of the theatre lobby looking sad. Sad on a ghost looked gaunt, frightful. Marina hadn't come back by to his surprise, he hadn't meant to scare her or the pretty sad girl. He flew over to the bar and up to sit on the very top of all the shelves near the ceiling next to the expensive liquor no one ever ordered. He could use a drink. A paperboy rode down the street throwing the daily news onto people's stoops, he paused in front of the theatre looking up at the marquee. Clive was immediately outside standing in front of his bike as he drew a paper from his satchel. He gently tossed it to the door, headline.

"Mutilated Body Found In Suggested Satanic Ritual: Does Clutter City Have A Serial Killer?"

Underneath photos of the girl from the night before along with bloody images of a gruesome crime scene. Clive screamed out and the marquee blew sending sparks into the street making the paperboy screech to a halt staring back in fear. A lady came out from one of the shops,

"Call the fire department!" He yelled. "Theatre is on fire again!"

Clive put his hands into his pockets and walked through the glass, across the lobby, back into the darkness of theater one.

CHAPTER 2IX

OSTEOPH⬥BIA

"Summer, please wake up." She heard a soft voice. "Please wake up." She sat up breathing in slapping at her chest to get off the roaches that had climbed onto her body. As she got up to run out of the basement skeletal hands grabbed at her ankles, slapping her to the ground and drawing her back towards the demonic sacrificial symbol. She screamed as her body bumped along the concrete floor scraping the backs of her legs.

Clive reached out his hands passing through hers. She ripped her taser out of her pocket and snapped it at the creature, it shrieked and let her go. She scrambled to her feet and they both ran up out of the darkness. The skeletal women from earlier now manifested as Blake and Marina's rotted bodies chased them out the front doors shrieking. Summer dove from the porch into the grass rolling back and staring into the house where the ghosts slammed the door.

"That's… that's what you see all of the time?" He shook his head, eyes wild with fear. Summer's bloody nose dripped onto her shirt.

"Let's get the hell out of here." She spun on her heel and took off, Clive behind her as she sped her way towards home. She went for a while until two miles later she found an ice cream shop stopping dead in her tracks.

"I need some sugar."

"Go for it, but uh, you may need something for your face…"

Summer ignored him, walking into the shop with her bloody nose she ordered a triple scoop lemon flavored ice cream from the shocked shopkeep. She grabbed a bunch of napkins on her way out. They sat in the park on a bench as Summer sadly licked her ice cream with her messed up face. A few passerby's stared at her in concern but she glowered at them and they moved on, Clive stared sadly at the sky.

"Do you want to talk about… what happened?"

Summer ate her cone and wiped at her face, getting the blood off. She recounted the gruesome details to him who's face crumpled into grief at hearing of Marina's end.

"No…" He said burying his head into his hands, ghostly tears leaking from his eyes and floating to dissipate into the air.

"I'm so sorry…" She pulled her knees up to her chest and stared at a blue moth as it landed on her boot.

"The paper… it didn't say anything about her. No one said anything at the theatre…"

"He must have done something with her body. Whatever he did… he made himself more powerful. It was like he… he absorbed her soul, both souls."

"And you're sure it's always on a full moon… just like in the movies?"

"Yeah…"

"When is the next one?"

Summer sighed, staring at the red ball of sun as it melted into multicolored clouds.

"Tomorrow night… except…"

"Except *what*…?"

"It's a super moon, a lunar eclipse. If he… if he finds a victim he could potentially be unstoppable."

"What does that mean?"

"He could do this endlessly, until this body goes and he gets a new one, as long as he can continue to harvest souls. Like a ghost on pcp. The host must have made a bargain with the demon for something. The demon uses his form to kill, and he, I assume, gets power or… I don't know what exactly, it must be manipulating him."

"And the… camera?"

"Maybe he's just fucking sick."

"He's acting like a demented director."

"Could be exactly what he is." Summer buried her head into her knees. Her mind was screaming something at her, her intuition trying to tell her something she couldn't quite understand.

"Hey do you see that?"

She looked up terrified into the trees. Clive pointed at something into the darkness and she peered seeing multicolored lights.

"I think that's the Scare Fair."

"The what?"

He got up and ran towards the woods, Summer slowly following his glowing form through the trees towards a large enclosure at the back of the flashing hustle and bustle. He pointed to a broken spot in the fence.

"They haven't fixed this shit since I was a kid."

Summer half smiled and crawled underneath as Clive flowed right through. On the other side he grinned at her as she stood, coming close to her seeing her freckles in the soft blue twilight. He peered into her eyes.

"What do you say we take a break?" His hand reached up to caress her cheek. It was cold, she couldn't help the soft purse of her mouth.

"That sounds... that sounds nice."

She stepped away from him towards the crowd, they immediately got lost in the foot traffic of gleeful families. Summer got a funnel cake and Clive teased her as she ate it. Various people in costumes, witches, zombies, skeletons, mummies, devils. A little girl in a skull mask ran up to her screaming bloody murder in her face. Summer stood in shock as she was chased off by a young vampire. Clive and her made knowing eye contact before heading for the Ferris wheel.

"We can get a good view of the city?" He said.

They got on and slowly rotated to the top where the wheel stopped. They stared into the sea of city lights, juxtaposing the sky like two sets of stars. The moon rose its giant orange body between them.

"Do you think everyone sees something different in the craters?" She asked.

"Like a Rorschach test?"

"Sure, what do you see?"

"A dragon sometimes. You?"

"A screaming woman."

"I can see that."

"I've always loved the moon." She said leaning onto the bar that separated her from the ground, tucking her hand into her chin. "When I was a little kid I used to think it was following me. Told my mom it was my best friend, went everywhere I went."

"Can't say I see it positively right now, more like an hourglass than a hunk of rock."

"I get it."

"I don't remember the first time I saw it…"

"You don't?"

"No, I mean it's just kind of always been there."

Leaning back, gently she moved her hand to touch his. It felt soothing, electric, in the unusually warm October air. Moving forward their lips gently locked. Neither feeling much more than a brush of a gentle breeze, but it was enough. The Ferris wheel started and they moved quietly to the ground, wandering their way through the crowd cracking jokes.

"Did you grow up here?"

"All my life, and after I guess. Crazy to see how everything has changed in a decade."

"The technology now is changing fast. Have you heard DVDs are replacing VHS?"

"I overheard some kids in the lobby talking about them. Hunter said they're expensive as fuck but I'll take that over the rewinding."

Summer looked over to see a man in a skeleton face mask with a camera held up to his blackened eye. A little kid ran into her hitting her hard in the stomach, when she recovered and looked away from the apologizing child the man was gone.

"You okay?"

"Yeah, just, nothing…" Summer shook her head. Another creepy vision.

They made their way back to her apartment, Summer got into some pajamas and crawled into bed.

"Hey, Clive?" He float through the door.

"Yeah?"

"Will you sleep with me?"

"You sure?"

"Yeah, I don't want to be alone."

Clive float over to the bed and rested next to her as if he were laying in a hammock, hands as pillows. He kept his eyes on the ceiling.

"Thank you."

"What do you think is going to happen when we find who did it?"

"We can drop the information to the police and leave."

"What do you mean?" He looked sad.

"You can come with me."

"Is that what you want?"

"You deserve more than this."

"You really don't think this is going to be like the end of Ghost, I get the light portal and poof?"

"I've never… I didn't want to tell you really, I just have *never* seen it. They usually just go back to where they were. I think that the idea of redemption after death? That's all in the way that you look at it personally, you'll feel what you want to feel. You'll send a man to jail for murdering you which is great, fuck that guy, but that's not the *way out* really. If there even is... one."

"So some souls are trapped, just trapped, in a two mile radius of where they die?"

"Some can wander, there aren't any rules."

"What about the old ghosts?"

Summer shook her head looking over at the wall so he couldn't see the fear on her face.

"That's... that's what... It's not a demon, the way you would think that we are fighting."

"What do you mean?"

"At first I thought it was just a man. Someone maybe with too much power that manifested into cruelty. This? What I saw in that house. Osseous, the real Osseous? A human ripped apart and fractured from birth until now, wild alive, more brutal in death. What will happen when the moon eclipses is something... primal. Something old. This been around a long time, and it can do things... things that would take centuries to manifest. If someone were to die a powerful psychic they could become something very good... or very, very, very bad."

"You're not strong enough to fight something like that, Summer. Don't be fucking stupid just leave."

"If whatever that is gets loose it could kill a lot of people. I've heard whispers of some, old souls that figure out how to... possess new bodies, they wander... and they kill."

"Ghost Invasion of the Body Snatchers." He reached out and touched her hand as she laughed, but but was a sad sound. She covered her eyes.

"We are going to need a plan."

"What we need is back up."

"Let me just call all my psychic, demon fighting, friends." She snipped.

"And what you really need is rest. Get some sleep, okay?"

"I'll try." She rolled over and cuddled close to his hip. He reached out a cool hand touching her hair, sad he couldn't feel it.

"Sweet dreams."

She woke in the dark, eyes wide, unable to move. Immediately her breath caught in her chest, sleep paralysis? She hadn't experienced this since she was a kid. The lamplight next to her flickered on. She made a noise, where was Clive? She got her neck to move and looked over, underneath the door a torrent of blood began to spill until it was a flood whooshing under her bed, out of it a horned creature rose from the crimson river. Skeletal hands ripped at the white fabric of her bed as it crawled up her body. Moving its exposed teeth to graze her face, empty sockets stared into her eyes.

"இறப்பு இல்லை. இறந்தவர்கள் இல்லை."

Summer couldn't scream. The light went out before flickering back to life, Clive hovered against the wall, eyes wide in fear. When she looked down the sinister bloody hand prints were all over her body and bed.

"You were… your eyes." He couldn't look at her.

By the time light was filtering through her curtains she had changed her sheets. Sitting in the living room Clive shook his head before breaking the silence between them.

"What the fuck was that?"

"Osseous. Delivering a message, "*There is no death. There are no dead.*'"

"This is fucking stupid. You can't handle this. You need to leave."

"I don't think I have a choice. Since this has started, I don't know if it will ever be over."

"You know what? You're weird! A total fucking freak! This whole… situation is stupid." He threw his hands into the air. "What am I going to be tethered to you until what? You find someone else and I'm just… your ghost best friend? Fuck off, Summer. Stay away from me! Never come back!" In a blink he was gone.

Summer sank to her knees staring at where he'd been sitting.

"Don't leave."

The apartment looked too sharp to her, the dark spots too dark and the beams of light not bright enough. She didn't want to be alone, how could he leave her like that?

That day she flipped through her occult book. Thinking of when she'd been drawn to it at an old shop and stolen it as a small child. She'd been reading it ever since, deciphering it's old pages of knowledge written in a thousand different languages that took years to piece together. She knew with it's guidance what she had to do. Just questioned her strength to do it at all.

All day she ate sugar, depleting her fridge. She took a long shower and changed into black pants, boots and a bright yellow shirt with a picture of the sun. Stuffing her bag full of what she needed she cast a last sad look back on her temporary habitat with it's too big windows and unlived in charm. The sun set on the city, a moon the size of the full sky rose into the air to replace it. It's screaming skull shaped cavities more prominent than she'd ever seen. She wanted so badly just to pretend it wasn't real and go back to bed. Leaving her apartment she heard a creak and looked over to see Velasquez peeking out.

"Hey, kid." She croaked. "We never got that dinner. I haven't been feeling the best." She coughed. "Where you rushing off to?"

"You think... Life moves pretty fast, huh?"

"Only way it's ever been for me. Even the moments you want to slow down."

Summer looked at the ground and back to her.

"We'll have that dinner when I come back tonight?"

Velasquez stared hard at her.

"Sure, kiddo. Whatever you say." She pulled cookies from the dark. "Take some."

Summer took a few smiling.

"Just what I needed. Secret weapon. See you, detective."

"Be seeing you."

Summer walked out the door. On the way to the theater she kept seeing Emma, Blake and Marina from the corners of her eyes. They were yelling something she couldn't hear.

She bought a ticket, ditching and dodging the torrents of people going to see the new Bone Demon 3. She found her way to the girls bathroom. Clive popped into the stall with her.

"You should leave." He yelled.

Summer looked down.

"No." She said, tightening her fists around her backpack strap.

Clive softened.

"Please leave, Summer."

She shook her head.

He shoved his hands into his pockets.

"I found… I found something today." He whispered looking at the ground, the look on his face, he was afraid.

"What is it?"

"It's… downstairs there's a door. I can't… I can't get through it."
He was shaking. "You shouldn't go down there. It felt wrong. It
felt really wrong."

"Show me where it is, Clive."

He floated through the bathroom and she followed. She
snuck past the staff and into a back room where Clive passed
through a door. Opening it she descended into a basement.

"These old theatres… some were made with speakeasies in the
back. We'd only had the place a couple of years and I never
thought to check for…" He shook his head. "Stupid." He walked
through the dark musty room covered with tons of stacked old
films, cardboard cutouts of movies and celebrities, broken
theatre items, and disappeared into the wall.

"Push it…" He called from the other side.

She did and it popped open revealing a dark hallway
draped in faded gold and green striped wallpaper. Cobwebs
and spiders had made this their home for a very long time but
you could tell someone had been in there recently. At the end of
it was a bright red door that made Summer stop in her tracks.
Clive was right it felt… evil.

"I don't think you should go in there."

"I don't think I have a choice."

She walked forward, Clive got in front of her but she
passed right through him.

"Don't." He said.

Twisting the ornate old knob, she shoved open the door. In the middle of the room were a myriad of stacked televisions in a tetrahedron shape each playing a different scene in the Bone Demon series combined with the footage of Blake, Emma and Marina being murdered. Shots of Summer in her home, at the graveyard, fair, theatre littered throughout. How long had he been following her? The televisions were arranged on top of the familiar demonic symbol, waterfalls of wax and dust dripped down their sides. In the corner sat four decrepit old bodies propped up their rotted eyesockets staring eternally at the horrific broadcast. She went to the corner and threw up.

"Summer watch ou…!" She felt something hard hit her in the back of the head, blood red darkness.

Clive recognized a man who had been aged by time, a kid he'd hired ten years before, the ticket clerk.

"Sam?"

The wild eyes of the brunette boy turned as if they heard him but he looked through him.

"If you're here, Clive." He said. "You'll get to watch."

Terror iced through his heart as he powerlessly watched him drag Summer to the middle of the room to the pentagram next to the demented pyramid. Clive flew through him punching his face over and over but nothing happened. He screamed and the screens around him flickered. Sam laughed, tying Summer's hands and legs.

"You fucking piece of shit!" He shouted.

Leaving her there Sam exited the room checking his watch.

"Not quite showtime." He said and disappeared.

"Summer, Summer for the love of god wake up."

But she was out cold, her blonde hair splayed over her resting face pushed uncomfortably against the harsh ground.

"Summer, seriously, please. Please. Please wake up."

Hours passed with her on the ground, the demented movies playing on loop next to him. Desperately he tried to untie her ropes, slap her awake, knock something over, anything but he couldn't. Eventually his panic was so overpowering he felt like he would be sick.

"Wake up. Wake up. Wake up." He said over and over trying to shake her.

"Unnnnh…" He heard her make a noise.

"Summer, dude, I need you to get up right fucking now. Get up."

He heard her whimper.

"Ow. Ow, ow." She said struggling against the ropes. "Clive?" She called out. "Clive." She was crying.

"I'm here." He came down and leaned in front of her face, her desperate eyes looking at him.

"I can't… I can't move." Her breath was catching in her chest.

"I tried, I can't get you untied."

"You have to go upstairs." She whispered. "Get someone's attention can you… have you tried going inside of someon…"

He heard footsteps coming down the stairs and he stood up standing over her body, arms out. Sam entered the room and threw a duffel bag on the floor. He took off his clothes, underneath a skeleton suit and grabbed a large satanic skull mask from his bag. He rose, slipping it on before turning his attention to Summer.

"Let's make some movie magic."

His movements were sharp and jutted in the scattering light of the candles as he crept towards her body. He reached out for her and Summer screamed.

"Don't touch me you fucking asshole!"

"I've been watching you." He whispered. "You're not like the others."

"Fuck you." She said staring up at the empty eyes of someone's stolen skull.

"You can see. See what I've done. Why I've done it. It told me, told me you were special. That we need you. That you're strong."

Summer looked over to Clive.

"He's here isn't he?" He said gleefully. "I knew he would be."

"Did you kill him?"

Sam pulled something from his pocket, a knife made of human spine.

"We needed him. For this. It could have been anyone… really."

"You killed him for no reason?"

"No, I didn't like him." He bent down and slowly cut her cheek making her cry out and him laugh. He licked her blood and shuddered.

"You are strong."

"Why are you doing this?" She whimpered.

Sam walked to the corner of the room turning on the multiple cameras set against the wall.

"Don't you see? I'm making the perfect movie. He promised me, if I gave him what he wanted, if I shared my body we would make the greatest horror film of all time."

"That's psychotic he... it is messing with your mind you're just... killing people..."

"Shut up!!" Sam yelled and ran at her hitting the ground next to her forehead with his fist. "It's *art.*" He shouted into her crumpling face. "When the moon eclipses we will get the best shot of all... your close up."

Clive disappeared. Upstairs he saw Hunter outside locking the doors he turned walking away from the theater.

"Sorry man but you kind of owe me this after you married my girlfriend."

Clive rushed outside and into his body just as he was about to step away from the marquee. He shuddered, looking as if he were going to throw up and wiggled around like his legs were made of jelly. His eyes went criss crossed and he fell to the ground.

Back down in the basement Sam had changed most of the broadcasts on the tv to multiple close up shots of the moon in real time outside.

"It's almost time." He said standing.

"You know it won't give you what you want? It's just manipulating you… if you stop I could try and untether you… he'll fully take over when he's done. It won't BE you anymore."

"We will be *one*, and I will be remembered as the greatest director of all time." He sighed dreamy, unhinged. He picked up a handheld camera decorated with skull stickers staring at it in a religious way. "I kept their souls tethered here. Til you came with enough raw power for them to reach you. They were whispering to you, I know it. Soon you'll be with them, no more escaping for any of you."

He pulled the knife from its hiding place and came over to her slowly slicing one wrist and then the other.

"If I don't cut your radial artery this could take quite a long time. I'll need more of you." He tapped his head, "This requires blood and your kinetic bone." He went over to the cameras and turned each of them on, setting them at different points in the room as Summer's blood slowly filled the riveted pentagram.

Hunter burst into the chamber screaming gutterily he ran at Sam swinging what looked like a giant old tripod. At the moment he made hard contact with Sam's skin Summer's blood completely filled the symbol, something changed in Sam. He seemed to immediately swell, larger, the harsh metal crumpled against him like paper.

"The living," He said, hitting Hunter sending him flying into the wall, his voice different, old. "Are pathetic."

Hunter hit his head and passed out blood trailing down the wall from where he'd impacted, his arm looked sickeningly bent. Clive crawled painfully up and out of his body uselessly staring at Summer bleeding out on the floor.

"Little, ānmā." His tongue extended licking her ear, but she was too weak to move. "You have been my favorite مستبصر in centuries. Your mind is so strong, your bones must be so beautiful." He caressed her middle, then her face.

Summer was whispering something under her breath.

"What are you saying?" He moved his head unnaturally to be next to her mouth. The light in Summer's eyes faded as the blood moon reached its peak. Her head falling softly to her side, her eyes open.

"Nooooo!"

Clive screamed running at Osseus he expected to run right through but he made contact hitting him full force sending him flying into one of his cameras. The demon stood shaking it off looking around the room in confusion. Clive hit him again, ripping his skeleton garb. Underneath his shirt Sam's bones had pushed up, swollen large, against his skin raising to show his skeletal frame in petrifying detail making him two sizes bigger.

He roared and ran for Clive but as he reached the middle of the pentagram he stopped as if stuck, unable to stab him with the spine dagger. The screens in the middle of the room flickered. The laughter of three girls flitted through the room, images of Emma, Blake and Marina's smiling faces warped through the screens before replacing them with desperate screaming. Slowly three pairs of skeletal hands broke through the television's water like static. Emma sopped out in a rush of river water followed by Blake and Marina oozing jelly like blood. They crawled across the floor, their broken bodies screeching and groaning, up Osseus' frame. They held his wrists and pulled back his head slipping their fingers into the empty bone sockets, ripping his horns making his head immovable.

Slowly the four corpses sitting in the chairs forced to stare at the eternity horrifying media came to life. Their bones cracking, they slowly started ricketing towards their killer. Clive went with them, taking the dagger made from his spine from the hand of Osseus. The demon bellowed in anger speaking in a language he didn't understand.

Clive plunged the dagger into his head breaking through the bone and into flesh. He watched as Osseus deflated becoming a bruised and empty version of Sam as the ghosts and skeletons ripped him to pieces his blood spraying the walls, TVs, cameras, spilling around them like an explosion of red. In the corner Hunter woke up, looking around him he shouted out in fear.

Clive turned around going to pick up Summer's bloody body, he felt the warmth fading from her skin. He pushed her eyes closed and held her to him for the first time, the last time.

Detective Velasquez stood in the underground room observing the mass of yellow tape, deep frown on her face. Her hair had grown back, color in her cheeks, three weeks cancer free. Doctor said it was a miracle. In the room they had cleared everything out and destroyed the demonic symbol in the middle of the floor. Velasquez touched where they had found Summer's body, the rush of warmth and peace made her eyes tear up painfully. She cursed herself under her breath thinking of the photos, how she hadn't stopped her from leaving. What the fuck had the kid been so mixed up in? Her apartment was empty, filled with occult items she had hidden for her so the department wouldn't know.

Had she killed this guy? Ripped him apart like that? Brave little thing. She left the room going upstairs to the overflowing theatre. People loved a good tragedy, a ritualistic murder was somehow a demented selling point for this place.

She looked over seeing a despaired young man sitting on a bench up against a mural of multicolored universes, a poster they'd put up for some up and coming sci fi movie. She shook her head, she'd seen him with Summer before they had passed she knew they'd been friends.

Clive stared out into the sea of swarming people, he'd felt like a shell since Summer had passed a month ago. He missed her. How long would he be trapped here like this? He wanted to die, disappear, but he was already dead. Had he done something to be punished? To be in the theatre forever?

He felt something warm touch his shoulder and looked over to see a glowing golden figure materialize into a familiar happy face.

"Let's get out of here." She said.

THE END?

About the Author

Michelle Skelton is a creepy crawler that lives in the Midwest, where the wheat grows high and people are weird. Her best friends include her sister, her dog and her car. This is the second book she's written in 2021, a part of her large scale Pulpaphobia horror series. Designed to be a never ending collection of short horror stories for adults, embodying the terrifying and cheesy spirit of the pulp horror and b horror that raised her. Aspiring comic book writer, filmmaker that wants to make community movies centering around Kansas and it's scary sunflower people.

Made in United States
North Haven, CT
03 July 2022

20920951R00062